Aiden

L.H. Gailen

Disclaimer

All the information in this book is to be used for informational and educational purposes only. The author will not account in any way for any results that stem from the use of the contents herein. While conscious and creative attempts have been made to ensure that all information provided herein is as accurate and useful as possible, the author is not legally bound to be responsible for any damage caused by the accuracy as well as use/misuse of this information.

Contents

CHAPTER 1

THE FALL OF A KINGDOM

The night is red with flames and smoke coming from burning houses; it goes so high up that it touches the night sky. Men, women, and children are running in all directions, trying to escape from the horror unveiled before their very eyes. The soldiers from two fronts – the village of Cremindale and the kingdom of Belbourgh are engaged in a fierce battle.

Cremindale is under attack, and soldiers wielding magical weapons are battling with one another. Belbourgh is trying to bring Cremindale to its knees, and its soldiers are steadily fighting back. But it is not enough. Their opponent's army appears to be stronger and is soon overwhelming them. Not sparing the children, women, men, and soldiers, the Belbourgh army subdues the village, killing anything and everything they come in contact with.

The kingdom of Belbourgh is at an advantage, as there's no one in Cremindale strong enough to contend with their magical abilities and weapons. Even their mighty king can't come close. If they were to fight Belbourgh about a century ago, they might have had the chance as the only person they deemed fit to counter Belbourgh's magical prowess died well over fifty years ago, leaving the kingdom almost helpless.

Moments later, the attacking army breaks through the castle gates, gaining access to the king's chamber. The cheering army sweeps through the castle walls, killing everyone in sight. Some people are pleading for mercy, while others defend themselves as the valiant soldiers they've been trained to be. The pleading and counterattack came to naught as the Belbourgh soldiers continued to slay them with no mercy. Although the valiant soldiers that stood their ground were killed, they died with honor.

The soldiers make their way to the throne room and find the village king sitting on his throne. They ask him to surrender his kingdom peacefully, but he refuses. Following his refusal, the soldiers make their way to attack him. As expected, the king puts up a fight and kills some of the men before heading for their leader. But, as he gets closer, the unexpected happens. The king of the village of Cremindale is suspended in the air like a commoner. Having no magical powers of his own, he is left with no choice but to resign to fate.

While the king is still suspended mid-air, a sorceress walks up to where he is and stands right before him. His eyes widen in disbelief, but before he can say anything, he is torn apart by the magical force surrounding him, killing him on the spot. The face of the leader of the Belbourgh army turns into a smirk as he stares at the former king's remains. The dismembered body lying before him would have been a Lord in his council had he accepted his proposal, but here he is, in pieces, with his blood coursing through the floor. The sorceress, a young maiden, interrupts his thoughts as she seeks instruction on the next line of action. The leader pauses for a while as silence engulfs the room. Then, after a brief moment of thinking, he orders the total extermination of all the royals and everyone related to the throne in the kingdom. The commander of the Belbourgh army bows his head to the order and leads his soldiers out.

Several meters away from the chaos in her kingdom, a woman in white garments beautifully laced with gold embroidery running over the fabric and a hood covering her head runs through a thick forest. She has a child in her arms and is accompanied by a man helping her up whenever she falls.

"Let's keep going; we don't have much time," the soldier would say, helping her up.

Their mission is to safely get her and the child far away from the chaos looming in the land and the inevitable death. The woman struggles to breathe and keep up with the man as they run through the forest. Upon noticing her struggle, the man takes the crying child from her arms to help ease her burden.

"We will soon be there; just a few more steps, and you will be safe." The man says as he urges her to keep moving.

The woman nods her head in agreement and quietly follows him. The thorns from the trees puncture and tear her once white garment as she walks between them, but she doesn't budge. She's more interested in her safety than the state of her beautiful garment. Finally, they reach a running river and attempt to cross to the other side. The soldier hands the child back to the mother and gets into the running water. As he turns around to help her cross, something hits them, sending them flying in different directions.

The attack comes so fast that it is almost unseen, but the soldier manages to deflect it with a counterspell. Although he couldn't completely deflect it because of the speed at which it came, he's able to reduce the damage. The woman is lying helplessly on the ground close to the river while the soldier is inside. A figure slowly and calmly walks towards them, obviously taking her time. Soon, the soldier emerges from the shallow water interrupting the shadow, which is now walking toward the woman. His attack makes the black shadow disappear as it sends shockwaves that crumble the ground beneath it.

The soldier hurriedly runs over to help the woman and her child up. He attempts to create a bridge over the running water so that they can cross to the other side, but an attack from the same shadow almost thwarts his attempt. However, he creates the bridge anyway and sets to battle this person that wouldn't let them be.

"Go straight up this path until you reach a place with two paths. Follow the one on your right and go down that path." The soldier instructs the woman.

"You'd find someone who'd take you to safety there." He assures her.

The soldier is careful enough to say all these to her hearing alone. The woman is petrified at what she's witnessing, knowing that someone will die protecting her and her child.

"Alright, I will go. May the High Father, Azathoth, be with you, always," she tells him with gratitude lacing her voice.

"Thank you! You should go now," he urges her on.

Holding her child tightly in her arms to avoid a fall, she crosses over to the other side.

A fight ensues between the soldier and the shadow but soon ends as the soldier suffers a defeat. The shadow clearly possesses more skills and power. Realizing this, the woman bursts into tears and becomes awash with fears for her child. She resumes her journey, which seems to have no end in sight. Finally, she reaches the point with the two paths and follows the one on her right, as instructed. Overwhelmed by exhaustion, she looks at her crying baby and tries to pacify him. She looks at him with eyes glistening with tears and then smiles. The baby soon stops crying and smiles back.

He hasn't even celebrated his second birthday, and his chance of survival is already looking bleak. His mother is convinced that the conqueror may have conquered their village, but they won't take the little world she has in her arms, at least, not on her watch.

After running a few meters, she finds a nearby bush. She uses her magic spell to cause her son to sleep. She then covers him up with the leaves from the bush and casts another spell to conceal his presence. This is to prevent anyone with magical powers from detecting or even finding him. When she's done, she stands up, wipes her tears, and starts making plans to continue her journey. Suddenly, she feels something coming towards her and then starts running.

The figure catches up with her in no time. She can't see who it is because it is dark, but she can tell that the figure is standing in front of her from the silhouette. The person stands in the dark, almost still.

"Show yourself, you monster!" she blurts out.

Like a command, the silhouette comes out of the shadow into the light, revealing the full appearance with nothing to hide. The person takes off the hood and mask covering the face, revealing her identity. The figure, the silhouette in the shadow, was no other person but the sorceress with the conqueror king.

"You!" the woman screams in shock.

"After all we've done for you and your father, this is how you repay us?" she asks.

"I'm sorry, but this is not what I intend for myself. I am simply following orders," the figure replies.

"Orders from a king who only sees you as a tool in his plans and not who you truly are," the woman asks in mockery.

"Enough!" The sorceress screams back at her clenching her fists in readiness for an attack. "Where is the child?" she asks, looking directly at the woman standing before her.

"You mean the boy you'd often play with whenever you come to the castle?" The woman asks rhetorically.

"Don't play games with me. Show me the boy or else..." the sorceress threatens, conjuring up a ball of flame over her palm.

"You have to go through me first," the woman says, with eyes furrowed in anger.

"You do know you are not as powerful as I am, right? I could easily end you with one hand tied behind my back," the sorceress says mockingly.

"I'd rather die than have you, savages, take my son away from me," the woman says, putting her fear aside.

"So be it!"

The sorceress charges at the woman with the flame she had made earlier, attempting to burn her. She throws the flame at her but the woman in white dodges it, leaping to another side. She makes a counterattack, casting a spell that dispels a force strong enough to push back the sorceress. The sorceress swiftly blocks it with a shield and casts a spell that makes her move fast enough to evade the subsequent attacks from the woman.

The sorceress successfully dodges the counterattack and then teleports behind the woman in white. She plunges her dragon-scale blade dagger right into the woman's left lung, ending her life.

As she stabs her with the dagger, it glows and emits a bright blue light that slightly brightens where they are. Soon, the light dims, and only a glow is left on the dagger. Then, she pulls out another dagger and slits the woman's throat, causing her to fall and die.

Standing over the woman's remains with blood oozing out of the open gash, she says, "I warned you."

She brings the dagger up to her chest and then recites an enchant that sends the glowing light on the dagger into her. The power surging through her causes her to clench the dagger's hilt tightly as she shakes. After gaining more power from absorbing the dead woman's magical powers, the sorceress proceeds to find the child.

She sends out energy, causing it to spread across the forest. Although the presence is felt faintly, she gets a sense of the presence of someone in the bush. She's convinced that the dead woman must have hidden the child nearby, so she sends another wave of energy, this time stronger than the last.

"Found you!" she exclaims with joy as she locates where the child is hiding.

She goes over to the bush where the boy is and tries to push it open to kill him. She knew her king would be proud of what she had done for him and the kingdom.

As she sets down to work, a voice reverberates in her head, distorting her thoughts, *"Orders from a king who only sees you as a tool in his plans?"* These were the dead woman's words, and the more she thought of impressing her king, the more the words kept ringing in her head. She eventually lets go of her plans as the dead woman's word had a stronger effect on her.

Moments later, a portal opens, and three men walk through it. They all look around, observing the events that occurred before proceeding to talk to the sorceress.

"Hmm, I see you killed her; that's very good. It was foolish of her to fight you, especially since she knew she stood no chance..." the man in the middle starts, "What about the boy? Where is he?" he continues.

"I do not know at the moment. I have searched the whole forest using my powers, yet I couldn't find him," she lies as she turns to them.

"Did you try again?" he asks.

"Yes, my lord. I sent out a spell that would pick up his presence twice and still couldn't sense anything," she replies.

Thinking about the situation, the men look confused. How can a woman with weak magical powers hide her son so well that the strongest magic-wielding sorceresses can't find him? Unable to solve the puzzle, the man asks the sorceress to return to the kingdom as Cremindale and its castles are now in ashes. He reminds her that they have to plan their next move, and the sorceress agrees with him. However, she seeks his permission to finish a task before returning to the Belbourgh. The man looks at her suspiciously but says nothing. Instead, he walks into the portal and leaves with the other two.

She immediately goes for the boy in the bushes and brings him out. She finds him sleeping, so she quickly teleports with him to a faraway place but still within the forest. She leaves the sleeping boy in one of the bushes and teleports back to where she was. Instantly, two men, tall and sturdy, show up at the place. They walk around the forest, searching the place with their eyes.

"Who are you, and what do you what?" the sorceress asks.

The men ignore her and continue with their search. She asks again, raising her voice a little perhaps they didn't hear the first time but again, they ignore her.

One of the men then casts a spell that forms dog-like creatures with glowing bodies. The creatures search through the forest, apparently looking for the young boy. When it is evident that the search was futile, they make the dogs vanish, and without saying a word, they leave using a portal.

The leader clearly wasn't satisfied with her duties and the way she handled the situation. He didn't trust her enough to believe that a powerful sorceress like her couldn't find the boy. And, to set things in order, he sent the other two sorcerers to find the boy. Luckily, she had already taken the boy from where they were to a place far away from possible danger and where other people could find him. She did this to fulfill the dead woman's dying wish woman – *"Please, save my son; he's all I have left."*

CHAPTER 2

NEW BEGINNINGS

After several hours of sleep, the young boy eventually wakes up late that night engulfed with fear. He begins to cry as he notices his mother's absence. His cry is so loud that he soon begins to attract the attention of passersby on that path. The disturbing cry stops a couple of people, but they flee upon seeing the child.

This goes on for a while until Phidel Willsworth and his wife, Jarian, go through the path. Phildel and Jarian are from Cremindale and have been married for over 12 years with no offspring. They are on their way home from a courtesy visit to a relative. They both sit in their small cart, discussing the sudden fall of another kingdom under the rule of

Belbourgh and the fate of the people in Cremindale. Phidel is seated in front, directing the horse, while Jarian is at the back, watching her husband. They talk in somber tones to avoid unnecessary attention. Suddenly, their conversation is interrupted by the cry of a child just ahead of their path.

"Do you hear that, Phidel?" Jarian asks in confusion.

"Yes, I do," he answers, looking as confused as his wife.

"I think it's coming from the bushes nearby," Jarian says.

"I think so too," he confirms. "Stay here; let me go check it out," he adds.

Phidel stops the horse to listen even more closely. He needed to confirm it was a child's cry they heard and not some creature in the forest. When the cry comes on again, he's convinced it's a child. He gets off the cart and walks over to where the cry is coming. Upon locating the place, he carefully opens the bushes, and to his surprise, there's a little boy all by himself.

"Good heavens, Jarian, it's a little boy," he calls out to his wife.

"Really? I would love to see this myself," she replies, jumping down from the cart and walking briskly towards her husband.

Jarian eyes widen as the little boy stops crying and stares at her. She bends down to the boy's face, looking at him with passionate eyes that exude the warm care of a mother.

"It's a little boy," she says softly.

"Yes. I wonder who kept him here." Phidel says with concern. "We should probably go," he says as he turns to leave.

"Are you insane? It's a little boy; we can't just leave him here," Jarian says convincingly.

"Okay, if that's the case, what should we do then? Take him with us?" He asks

Looking at Phidel with compassion and a smile on her face, Jarian nods her head, answering his question.

"What? You can't be serious, Jarian. We don't know this boy or where he's from, and we don't know..."

"It's okay, Phidel, I am the one that wants him, and I want to take him home with me, with us,"

"Oh no, this is a bad idea, Jarian,"

"You worry too much. Everything will be alright," Jarian says with conviction.

She bends over the boy again, and this time, she carries him into her arms. She looks at him and wipes his tears with her palms.

"You are safe now; you are safe with me," Jarian says as they return to the cart.

Phidel walks behind them, looking at his wife in amusement. She carefully puts the boy in the back seat before hopping right next to him. She wraps him in her warm embrace as she settles in. Phidel walks over to her, still insisting that taking the boy along with them is a bad idea.

"What if the person who puts him there comes back for him," he asks

"And what if there isn't anyone coming to pick him up, Phidel? Should we still leave him here? Are you not happy that we've finally found a child we can raise as ours?" Jarian blurts out.

"That's not what I mean, honey,"

"Then, what do you mean, Phidel? What?"

"I'm just saying... Are we going to raise this child?"

"Yes, we will. He has no one, I believe, so we will take him with us,"

Phidel goes silent, thinking of what his wife has just said. He looks at the little one in Jarian's arms with a face that has crumbled from worry. He darts his eyes from one point to another before looking at the boy again, and this time, he stares for a while. Then, like magic, his face starts to brighten as his eyebrows unfold. His crumbled face starts to come alive as his lips form a smirk and then a half smile. The boy looks at him and smiles too. Phidel's face is fully alive now, following the realization that Jarian might just be right about the whole thing. It may just be that Azathoth has given them a son, a son of their own, one who would come and make their home feel warm and complete.

These thoughts run through Phidel's mind as he weighs his wife's decision. He looks at Jarian playing with the boy and sees how happy she is to be with the child. He has never seen her this motherly before, and now, he can't deny her happiness with the boy. He thinks for a while longer before agreeing to her request.

"Alright, Jarian, we will go with the child," he says, extending his hand to Jarian, who cups her palm in it.

"Thank you," Jarian looks up to him with teary eyes.

"Don't even think about it," Phidel teases.

Jarian lets out a chuckle before wiping her tears. She places her hand on Phidel's right shoulder as they continue their journey home.

After riding for a few more miles, they eventually arrive at their home. It is a middle-sized house with a brown rooftop and beautifully painted cream. They have obviously made good use of the large land space surrounding the house. The land space contains a barn, livestock pen, and four horses.

The little boy had fallen asleep before they got home. So, while Phidel unpacks, Jarian carries him to their room to help him sleep better.

"You must have had a rough night but don't worry; you can sleep well now," Jarian whispers to the sleeping boy as she makes him comfortable.

"You are letting him sleep in our room now? Really?" Phidel questions as he comes into the room.

"That's right. I want him to be with me. He's only a child, and I can't let him sleep alone," she says, lying next to the boy.

"Where am I supposed to sleep, then?" he asks.

"Phidel, there are other rooms in the house. You can sleep in one of them," she says, yawning.

Phidel is disappointed at the turn of events, and since he can't do much, he makes his way to another room. Ignoring her husband's disappointing look, Jarian brings the child close to her as though afraid that he will vanish while she sleeps. She holds him close like a precious gem. She opens her eyes slightly only to catch a glimpse of her child faintly. She smiles at his peaceful sleeping face before she drifts into sleep.

CHAPTER 3

NEW BELBOURGH

The victory of the Belbourgh kingdom has forced the people of Cremindale to adopt the Belbourgh's culture and become a part of the kingdom. They now eat their food, wear their clothes, participate in their festivities, and follow the Belbourgh's rules to the latter. It has become evident that the Belbourgh King has succeeded in erasing anything that resembled Cremindale, wiping its culture out from the face of the land.

When the siege at Cremindale occurred, its vanquisher came under heavy rebuke from the remaining four kingdoms – Lildephia, Midelia, Handale, and Winxforte, for his actions were contrary to the pact they all shared and agreed on.

The kingdoms had earlier agreed that no other kingdom should attack another in a quest to conquer it and its people. However, following the King's disobedience, the other kingdoms have threatened to wage war against Belbourgh and take the kingdom away from him unless the King moves his army out of Cremindale. But there is a problem – no other kingdom can face the Belbourgh army as it is now the strongest of all the other kingdoms, thanks to their victory in Cremindale.

The King of Belbourgh justified fighting and seizing the village of Cremindale. He claimed that the village needed a better king who could make the kingdom great. And after thinking it through, he realized that merging his kingdom and the village was the best option. Even though he tries to convince the leaders of the other kingdom that his decision came from a good place, they disagree with him. Having known the King for so long, they can tell that the actual reason he went to war with Cremindale is a result of greed. Although Belbourgh is one of the largest kingdoms in the land, he still seeks to expand his territory and gain more control.

The displeasure of the other kingdoms forces them to call for a meeting where the King of Belbourgh makes a proposition. The King's proposition to the other four kingdoms contained two options. The first option involves an attack from the other kingdoms after 17 years. The King claims they'd have a considerable advantage over his kingdom because the Belbourgh army's magic will be weakened by that time. Belbourgh is located on a land with immense magical energy, and it has a mountain from which its army can draw magical energy, making their power and strength great. This has been the reason for all their victories and why they are the most feared. But, during a half-moon, this power is blocked and cannot be used till the duration of the half-moon passes. The night is shorter during this period, and as such, the other kingdoms stand a chance to defeat Belbourgh. However, the second option involves the other kingdoms swearing their allegiance to the Belbourgh kingdom or getting crushed.

The leaders of the other kingdoms thought long and hard on both options and concluded that the first option was preferable. They knew that the Belbourgh army got their immense magical energy from their land and that the half-moon would weaken it, if not completely make it useless. The Belbourgh army was known for their tact on the battlefield, so this was the perfect opportunity for them all. The leaders left the meeting, going to prepare their men for war. Little did they know that the Belbourgh King had other things planned out. Never on his watch are they going to take Belbourgh away from him.

CHAPTER 4

AIDEN

"Wake up, Aiden," Jarian says as she gently pats her son on the shoulder

"Mother, don't you think it's too early?" Aiden asks with a smirk

"Don't play with me, young man. You know the animals in the barn won't feed themselves, right?" she asks.

"Besides, don't you know what day it is today?" she adds, smiling.

"The day you let me sleep as much as I want," he pouts as he teases his mother.

"Don't be silly, son, get up," she commands

"Alright, mother. You win. I'm up."

"Good morning, mother," he says as he sits up to face his mother.

Jarian stays silent for a moment as she stares at her son. She looks at him so lovingly that one can easily tell how much she loves him. Aiden stares back but looks away almost immediately.

"Good morning, son," she replies, still staring.

"You are giving me that look again, mother," he says with a smile

"Why shouldn't I? You are my son, and I love you," she says, placing her right hand on his face. As she speaks again, she caresses his face with her thumb, "You've grown so much."

"Yes, I know, and I love you too." He says, stroking his mother's hand. Aiden uses their little mother and son moment to present a request that he has been stalking on.

"Mother, I'd like to go to the Linix with my friends in three moons. Since I'm seventeen now, I believe I can go," he adds with a pleading face.

"But son, isn't that place called Linix Death Ground? His mother asks with a frown.

"I hear people perform a lot of dangerous magic tricks there. I even heard two people got hurt from miscasting a spell," her voice is full of concern as she continues.

"Yes, but I wouldn't try any of their tricks when I get there. Trust me; I won't do anything stupid," he says convincingly. Then, when his mother doesn't respond, he asks, "can I go?"

"I will think it through," she says after a deep sigh

"Huh, mother. The event holds once a year, if I miss it now, I'll have to wait till next year, and I don't want that to happen.

Please, I assure you I will be careful," Aiden continues to persuade his mother.

"Alright, you can go," she says as she finally gives in.

"Yes!" he says, throwing his hands up in victory. "You are the best mother in all five kingdoms. Thank you so much, mother," he adds.

Jarian watches as her son scampers around the room, getting ready for the day. Seeing how happy and energetic he is moving around because she agrees to his request brings flashbacks of when he was younger.

One memory that struck her was Aiden and Phidel's market experience when he was only six years old. It was a fine market day, and the both of them had gone to get supplies for the house. Asides from the groceries they needed, Phidel wanted to get a new pair of boots for his son. Aiden has always been fascinated by the market. He loved seeing the colorful display by the traders and the scent of flowers. He also enjoyed watching the villagers show off their magical prowess. He marveled at the tricks and how the villagers used their magical abilities to entertain their audience.

The highlight of accompanying one or both of his parents to the market was playing with magical creatures such as the griffon (a cat with the wings of a hawk and can fly as fast as an actual hawk). It has been his long-time wish to own one, but the griffons in Belbourgh were too expensive.

That fateful day, Aiden and his father were working towards a grocery stall when a man deliberately bumped into them, pushing his father aside. Although Phidel tried to dismiss the event, the man still went ahead to challenge him.

"Don't you have eyes to see where you are going?" The man asked in a loud voice.

"That wasn't my fault. It was you who bumped into us." Phidel replied softly but confidently because he knew he was telling the truth.

Phidel's response seemed to trigger the angry man as it was contrary to his expectation. So, the man pushed him again, but this time to the ground. Angrily, Phidel got back on his feet and attempted to hit the man, but the man was quick to cast a spell to suspend Phidel in the air before he could reach him. Satisfied with the result, the man advanced toward him, laughing. At that point, the villagers had started gathering to watch.

The man got to where Phidel was hanging, which was only a few meters above the ground, and started punching him. Sadly, no one could interfere because none of them was strong enough to fight off the man. They knew him to be a troublemaker, and unless a person's magical energy matches his, there's no way to challenge him. Yet, Aiden charged at the man and held onto his leg. Seeing this, the man laughed hysterically before shaking the boy off like a rodent.

Phidel was among the numerous villagers with no magical ability. Therefore, all he could do was struggle to break free even though it didn't make any difference. The man laughed at his struggle and punched him some more. The numerous punches made Phidel bleed from his nose. Aiden's anger increased with each punch, and when he couldn't hold back the public humiliation anymore, he made an enchantment which turned out to be a spell. It was a single spell that caused the man to fly, crashing into a merchant's wares. The spell contained a special force designed to push an opponent away. However, one can control the force. In Aiden's case, he couldn't exactly control it, so the spell hit the man with an overwhelming force that knocked him out. In that instance, the man's magic shook off and lost its hold on Phidel, who dropped to the ground. The event was a shock because neither Aiden nor his parents knew he had such abilities. It was his first time casting a spell, and his parents, especially his mother, were overly excited.

"Mother, I would like to dress up now." Aiden's voice jerks his mother back to reality. She smiles as she looks at the young man in front of her. She couldn't deny that he gave her the warmest feeling in the world.

"Oh, yes, I will leave you now, but don't be late, okay?" she says as she walks out of his room.

"Alright, I won't," he replies

As soon as his mother leaves the room, Aiden makes an enchantment that takes him off the floor and changes his clothes for him. The spell typically takes off the one he had on and puts on new ones. He's able to do this because he's an eleventh-level magic wielder.

There are fifteen levels used to ascertain a person's magic power and all five kingdoms use it as a unified magic level gauge. Anyone can be in any of them, depending on their level of magical energy. Aiden could shoot himself to the eleventh level due to his immense magical energy. But he couldn't easily reach level fourteen or fifteen because he lacked proper knowledge, mastery, and skill in handling some complex magic spells and techniques. Despite that, a lot of people still envy his current position.

Aiden makes his way into the main living area as soon as he's satisfied with his appearance. He walks into the room expecting to see his parents, but no one is there. Surprised by this, he goes into the kitchen to check on his mother but doesn't find her or anyone else there. He's puzzled at this point, so he goes to their room to look for them but still doesn't find them.

"We should be having breakfast now, so where are they?" He thinks out loud as he makes his way back to the living area

"Mother! Father! Where are you?" he screams as he steps outside the house, searching for his parents.

"Weird, I swear I could hear them a while ago," he adds as he returns to the house.

"Surprise!!"

"Oh, Azathoth, you all scared me," Aiden says, smiling as he quickly regains his composure.

"I hope we didn't scare you too much?" his mother asks, looking at him intently and cupping his face in her palms.

He shakes his head, "no, mother. I'm okay and happy that you all pulled this up for me. Wow, this is a lot!" he says ecstatically.

"It's the least we could do, Aiden. Happy birthday," a voice from behind answers. The owner of the voice walks forward to hand him a present.

"Thank you so much, Meeryn," Aiden says, collecting the present from her.

Meeryn is one of the maidens from Belbourgh. She is Aiden's friend, and they've known each other since he was nine. She is one of those girls you can easily call 'pretty.' She has dark hair, dark eyebrows, sea-green eyes, a small nose, and full lips. Her personality is laudable too. She's resourceful, compassionate, and always willing to help others. Mareeyn is an intelligent girl; she can typically find her way through any situation. She possesses average magical energy and can use it skillfully. Having known Aiden for so long, she developed a crush on him. It's one of the reasons she sticks out a lot for him. Unfortunately, this stirs up rumors about being in a relationship with him in their neighborhood.

"Happy birthday, son," Phidel says as he hugs Aiden.

"You are growing into a fine young man, and I am proud of you, always," he adds.

Aiden and his father stare at each other with warm eyes as gratitude runs over their faces.

"Enjoy your party, son," Phidel says as he pats him on the shoulder before walking away from his side. He walks up to his wife, who wraps her hand around his waist in a brief hug.

"We have a present for you, Aiden," his mother announces as they both turn to face Aiden, whose face lits up with anticipation.

"Okay, what is it?" he asks with excitement.

His parents give each other a knowing look before his mother answers, "Give me a few minutes; I will be right back," she says, leaving the room.

Just then, another of Aiden's friends walks up to him and engages him in a conversation.

"11th level powers, yet, you couldn't even detect our presence in the living area. What a pity," his friend says mockingly.

"Yeah, I might not have been able to detect it this time, but I assure you it will be different next time," says Aiden.

"Uh-huh, I believe you," he says, eyes darting around the room. Finally, his eyes fall back on the celebrant, "Happy birthday, Aiden," he adds.

"Thank you very much, Himmel," Aiden replies.

Himmel Daegon is Aiden's longest and closest friend. They've been friends since Aiden was five. Aiden, Himmel, and Meeryn share a wonderful friendship. Although Himmel isn't as bright as the other two, he has a strong spirit that's resilient enough to crack the hardest stone. He is a 6'4 feet tall and strong fighter. His father and brothers trained him to be a formidable fighter right from when he was seven. Himmel has brown eyes, hair, and a muscular body due to his numerous training. Like his other two friends, he has magical abilities. Repulsive and destructive spells are his area of specification because he believes they put down one's enemies faster and harder. Himmel trains Aiden on fighting.

Jarian's reappearance interrupts their conversation. She returns to the party room dragging a box-like object across the floor. The room is filled with hush tones and gasps. Everyone but Phidel stares at the woman intently as if they'd get a clue of what she has with her. But unfortunately, the object is fully covered with a grey veil leaving no clues. Aiden walks up to his mother to assist her with the dragging but is taken aback by what happens. The object suddenly elevates from the floor and hangs in the air. Eyes widen, and mouths fall open at the sight of this. Jarian mouths a 'thank you' to her son upon realizing his initial gesture.

"What is this?" Aiden asks, eyeing the object suspiciously

His father cuts in just before his mother can speak. "Well, this is something you've wanted to have for a long time now," he says.

"Okay," Aiden says, looking over his shoulder at the friends behind him. "Can I take the veil off now?" Aiden asks.

"Sure," his parents say in unison.

Aiden takes off the veil with the speed of light. His eyes widen as his jaw drops in disbelief. He darts his head from the animal in the medium-sized cage to his parents for a few seconds before he regains his voice.

"Holy Azathoth! It's a griffon! Guys, it's a griffon! Oh my goodness!" Aiden screams for joy. "Thank you so much, father. Thank you so much, mother," he says, hugging his parents.

"You are welcome, Aiden," his mother replies, almost in tears.

"Oh, mother, not again..." Aiden gives her a tight hug.

"I'm sorry, son, it's just that I get emotional sometimes."

"You are always emotional," Aiden says, releasing her from his grip.

"No, I'm not,"

"Errm, you are, my dear," Phidel says with a smile.

"What? Is no one going to have my back here?" she shifts her gaze from her husband and child. "Who will help me tell these men that I'm not always emotional?" Jarian asks, looking into the crowd.

There's murmuring as everyone looks away almost immediately to avoid eye contact with her. Their attitude suggests that the situation is awkward. However, they are all smiling at her denial.

"Emotional or not, you are my wife and our son's mother. Nothing can change that," Phidel says.

He wraps his hands around her and places a soft kiss on her lips. The crowd gags as the children pretend to cover their eyes.

"Must you two do this here?" Aiden asks with a bright smile on his face.

"Oh! Stop being silly, Aiden. You know I love your father," his mother responds, returning the smile.

"I love you, too," Phidel replies, kissing her again.

"Let's leave them to enjoy their party while we go to our room to have our fun," he says playfully.

"Alright then, I like where this is going," Jarian says, with a tender tone accompanied by a wink.

"In here, really?" Aiden laughs as his parents leave the living area for their room.

The guests gather around the celebrant, talking, playing games, and having fun. Aiden leaves the room for the kitchen to get some snacks, drinks, and food for everyone, including the griffon. Before he leaves, he lets the griffon out of the cage to spread its wings, and it does just that.

"Whoa! The wings are huge, and it's already taking up the space here," Himmel exclaims.

"It's a big one. I wonder how old it is," Meeryn says

"Ah, I don't know. Say about five months or slightly above that. What I do know is that griffons grow quickly and can reach their full size in about a year," Aiden tells them. "Come on, girl, let's go get something to eat," he beckons to the creature.

Meeryn joins Aiden in the kitchen while he's still trying to sort out their food. He notices a reflection, so he looks behind to see who it is.

"Hey, Meeryn, came to lend a hand?" Aiden asks.

"Yes. I can't leave you doing all the work, right?" Meeryn asks flirtatiously.

"Yes, sure. Here, take these meatballs and this bottle of wine with you," Aiden tells Meeryn.

"These meatballs look yummy; looking at them makes me hungry already," she says with a smile.

"Well, wait till you eat them,"

Aiden checks a counter in the kitchen, searching for some fish for his new pet. He eventually finds some and puts it on a wooden plate.

"Here you go, girl, some fish," he puts the plate in front of the creature. He could tell that the griffon had been patiently waiting for the food.

Back in the living area, they start talking about the tryouts into the Magic Corps in the kingdom. They aspire to get into the institution's highest and most prestigious corps, but they know it'd require a lot of hard work.

Every year, the Earlmond Magic Institute conducts its recruitment exercise for potential sorcerers and sorceresses. The successful candidates represent the Institute in tournaments and act as security agents in the kingdom. So, the Institute only considers the best in the land. There are five corps in the Institute, each based on power levels. This means that entry into each corps will depend on one's power level and skills. The highest and most prestigious corps is the Fremin Magix Corps. It houses some of the best sorcerers in all five kingdoms. Fremin Magix Corps has the best techniques in the use of magical weapons, making it the most preferred choice for aspirants. Therefore, the entry is highly competitive.

"You've heard that Earlmond Magic Institute will be recruiting soon, yes?" Himmel asks.

"Yes, and I'm excited," says Meeryn. "I heard that your sister is in one of the lower corps in the institute, the third corps," she adds.

"You're right. But that's my sister. As for me, I'll become a member of the Fremin

Magix Corps, so I'll be able to use some nice weapons," Himmel boasted.

"That's good. I hope for the same too. Being a member commands a lot of respect in the kingdom," Meeryn says.

"Of course! It's the greatest corps, and it has some of the best and most powerful sorcerers in the world," Himmel points out.

"And sorceresses, too," Meeryn adds.

"Yes, and sorceresses too. Whatever," Himmel says, rolling his eyes. This act gets him a playful knock on the head from Meeryn.

"There are great sorceresses in the Fremin Magix Corps too. I have heard of one who's so good that she makes the men look like amateurs. Only a member of the council elders can match her magic usage and fighting techniques." Meeryn says with admiration.

"I even heard she was able to save the people from the kingdom of Winxforte from wild and magical beasts with immense strength, like the Godenhorg that was killing the people. She singlehandedly fought against the beasts because the remaining team members weren't powerful enough. She used a spell that wasn't popular to weaken the beasts before using her sword to kill them." Meeryn paused to look at Himmel's face. Then, satisfied with the admiration in his eyes, she continues. "And now, do you know her rank in the institute?" Meeryn asks.

"What rank?" Himmel asks in anticipation.

"The rank of a general. That's how good she is," Meeryn answers.

"Whoa! That's so impressive, Meeryn." He smiles.

"See, I told you there are cool sorceresses in the Fremin Magix Corps, too," she says with contentment.

"I can't wait to get in there," Himmel says with optimism.

"Me, too," Meeryn says.

"Hey, why aren't you saying anything, Aiden?" Himmel asks, picking up a meatball and glaring at his friend.

"Oh, me? Don't bother. It's nice listening to both of you talk." Aiden replies, giving a tight smile.

Himmel and Meeryn exchange looks. They wonder why Aiden didn't contribute to any of their discussion about the Institute.

"Aren't you excited about the tryout?" Meeryn asks Aiden in a low voice, sipping from her cup.

"Well, I can't say I am. The thing is, I've never given it a thought before, so I don't know what to think," Aiden answers genuinely.

"Oh, that's okay. But—"

"Oh, that's okay." Himmel mimics Meeryn as he cuts in,

"What do you mean by that's okay, Meeryn?" He continues without waiting for her answer. "No, it's not okay. Not okay, Aiden. You want to tell me you have never dreamt of gaining entry into the Earlmond Magic Institute, the biggest magic Institute in the world?" Himmel asks with wide eyes.

"It's the only Institute in the world. And thanks a lot for cutting me short, Himmel," Meeryn eyes him.

"Of course!" Himmel replies, ignoring Meeryn's sarcasm.

"Calm down, guys. I know about the institute and how great it is. I just haven't considered becoming a member. I just want to live," Aiden says, putting a biscuit in his mouth.

At that point, it hits Meeryn and Himmel that their friend may not have as much regard for the institute as they do. It has been their childhood dream to join the institute. They'd often fantasize about being inside, wearing their magic ropes and uniforms, training under the best trainers in the world, and set off to fight mythical beasts in faraway lands. They were so fascinated by the activities that it became more than a dream. It was a reality they were willing to live. How could Aiden trivialize something as solemn as that? Himmel is more disappointed as Aiden's indifference hits him the most.

"You have got to be kidding me, Aiden. By Azathoth's beard, you are kidding, right?" Himmel asks to confirm if Aiden was pulling their legs.

There's a brief silence.

"Yes, I was kidding, guys. You need to see your faces," Aiden says sarcastically as he laughs.

"Oh, High Father, I thought—"

"No, I wasn't kidding, Himmel. I meant what I said," Aiden continues, interrupting Himmel.

"Whoa, this is a new one for me. For an institute every person wants to get in, it is a surprise that you don't want any of it," Himmel says when he finds his voice.

"But, your magic energy is on the eleventh level. That means you are more than capable of being selected. Imagine what it would mean for you and your family. You could even attain the highest level of magic if you join them, becoming a master-level sorcerer," Meeryn tries to convince him.

"Master level sorcerer," Himmel repeats, stressing the last word

"I don't know, guys. I mean, I have a lot going on for me here. I have school, work, my father's business, and my mother," Aiden says, lowering his head at the mention of his parents. "And, I don't think I can leave them right now," he adds.

"Hmm, if that's the case, buddy, I wish you the best. For me, Earlmond Magic Institute is the place to be." Himmel says in what is supposed to be a consolation. He grins as he puts a biscuit into his mouth.

"Absolutely," Meeryn says as she agrees with Himmel. "And, we would always come to visit you, Aiden," she adds.

"That is when we are accepted," Himmel corrects.

"Yes, we will be accepted, dumdum. Be positive," she says, teasing Himmel.

"I am," Himmel replies.

Aiden laughs and urges them to eat the food in front of them before they move on to other activities. They agree with him and start eating as they discuss other things.

***

The night sky is a beauty to behold. There are shimmering dots of light cutting through the dark sky. The streets are empty as the men, women, and children have returned to their homes. Some animals are back in their burrows and hiding places, while some are out to hunt. There are lamps in many houses, and families are getting ready to have dinner or retire for the night.

A wife is nagging at her husband over food insufficiency. She screams at the top of her voice, calling him out for his irresponsibility. She even threatens to leave with their two children if nothing changes. The man blames his low artifact business patronage for his financial instability, but his wife turns a deaf ear. Tired of her nagging, he leaves the house amidst his children's plead. He runs into a man chasing a bread thief but doesn't budge. His family is at the edge of breaking, so he can't be bothered by a mere bread thief.

On the other hand, Aiden's family is getting ready for dinner. Phidel is going through some scrolls, Jarian is preparing the food, and Aiden is setting the table. Everyone takes their seats once everything is in place as Jarian serves the food.

"What about that business proposal you told me about, Phidel? Has Lord Norlan accepted it yet?" Jarian asks her husband.

"Oh! I almost forgot, yes. He has agreed to have me make a stone sculpture of him and two of his sons," Phidel replies happily.

"Wow, that's nice, father," Aiden says

"That's great. I am so happy for you, my love," Jarian says before kissing her husband. "But why does he want to sculpt just two of his sons? Doesn't he have like two more?" she asks, perplexed.

"He said he wants to use it to honor his two sons who made it into the highest corps in that magic institute, the Fregim Magic Corps." Phidel replies.

"It's the Fremin Magix," Aiden corrects.

"Oh. But, that's big, you know?" Jarian asks as she serves Aiden

"Yeah, it is," Phidel and Aiden answer in unison.

"Everyone in the kingdom seems to be talking about that institute. The men, women, and even children have something to say about it. If it's not the institute, then it is the corps. I hear many young men and women talk about wanting to be a part of the highest corps because it brings a lot of honor and shows how powerful they are." She adds as she settles to eat her food.

"Yes, th tryouts are in a few days, so many people are excited," Phidel says, making himself comfortable before digging into the sweet potato and chicken in front of him.

"Come to think of it, Aiden, why don't you try it out and see. Then, maybe, you might get selected," his mother suggests.

"I don't know. This is not something I would like to do. Besides, I'm happy the way I am," Aiden tells his mother, putting a chunk of food into his mouth.

"I know, but it wouldn't be bad to give it a shot. After all, you are a level eleven sorcerer," she says, looking at Phidel, who nods his head in agreement with her statement.

"It wouldn't be a bad idea having a son who becomes a powerful sorcerer himself, you know? And your entrance to the institute might just get you there," she adds, digging into her chicken.

"And, who knows, we might finally get the respect we deserve in this kingdom," Phidel adds.

"I can't believe we are having this discussion right now," Aiden says, surprised that his parents want him to participate in the tryouts.

"Just think about it, Aiden. Think about how people will treat us when you join," his mother urges.

"Especially when you make it into the highest corps, people seem to like it a lot. I hear it has some of the most powerful sorcerers and sorceresses there," Phidel says.

"And you could be one of them, doing great things for the kingdom," his mother adds convincingly.

"Alright, Mr. and Mrs. Willsworth, I will think about it," Aiden says with a forced smile.

His parents want him to join the institute, and he wouldn't want to disappoint them, but again, he's not convinced he wants to join.

"That's the spirit, son. May the High Father, Azathoth, be with you, always," his mother says, lifting her hands to the sky.

Aiden looks at his mother and smiles at her cheerful face and bright eyes at the thought of him joining the institute. Then, he looks over at his father; he's happy too, eating his food and nodding his head. Aiden doesn't know if it's because he agreed to consider the tryouts or if it's the food he is eating. But whichever it is, his happiness is all that matters.

Later that night, Aiden lays on his bed, thinking about the day's event. His mother's words keep flashing through his mind, "*May the High Father Azathoth be with you, always.*" He feels he has heard those words before, but he couldn't recollect. Finally, after several minutes of racking his brain, a faint image flashes through his mind. He sees a woman in white, her face is covered with a hood, and a man is standing in front of her. He doesn't see the man's too, but he hears the woman say the exact words his mother said to him at dinner. He thinks for a while and soon finds himself falling asleep. He shrugs off the thought and turns to blow out his lamp. He stares at the ceiling and imagines himself in the institute. Not long after, he sleeps off with a smile on his face.

CHAPTER 5

DECISIONS MADE

It's a bright day, and the Willsworth are preparing for the task ahead. Phidel and Jarian are in the living area having small talks while waiting for Aiden to join them. Phidel has a client to sculpt for before noon while his wife is going to visit a friend, after which she'd go to her pottery stall at the market. Fully dressed for school in a black leather long sleeve shirt, brown pants, and black buffalo hide pair of shoes, Aiden joins them.

"Good morning, mother. Good morning, father," he greets, beaming with smiles.

"Good morning, son. I hope you had a good night's rest." His mother asks as she gives him a brief hug.

"I sure did," Aiden replies, taking a loaf of bread from the breakfast set before him.

"Good morning, son. How are you?" his father asks.

"I'm fine, thank you," Aiden answers before forcing another loaf into his mouth.

His mother takes note of this as she puts down her cup. "You seem to be in a hurry, son. What's wrong?" she asks, with worry written over her face.

"Yeah, I'm late already. We have fight practice this morning, and I cannot afford to miss it," he replies.

"That's good," his mother says.

"Go easy on them, son. Try not to break their legs but knocking off their teeth should be enough," Phidel jokes with a grin.

"Phidel?" Jarian calls, hitting him on his shoulder playfully

Aiden smiles, "I won't, father." "I need to go now, bye." He adds as he stands to his feet. He teleports out of the house before either of them replies.

"Oh, he's gone," his mother says in disappointment

"He did say he was in a hurry," Phidel reminds her.

Jarian shrugs as they continue eating in silence. A few moments later, Aiden teleports back into the house and almost startles his mother.

"You need to knock before showing up, young man. You almost got me," she says, eyeing him.

"I'm so sorry. I forgot to tell you both something, but it's going to be quick," Aiden says in one breath.

"Okay, what is it?" His parents ask in unison.

"I've decided to participate in the Institute's tryout, okay, bye," Aiden says, vanishing again.

"Okay. That's great," Phidel says before realizing Aiden's disappearance.

Jarian would have been ecstatic had Aiden stayed a little longer, but he disappeared into nothingness before she could even find the words to say to him. Notwithstanding, she's happy he will finally use his powers the way she had always wanted him to – defending the land and joining the brave fighters to take Cremindale back from Belbourgh, restoring its independence.

***

Aiden makes it to school and rushes to the fighting class with every speed in him. He would have used his teleporting powers to the class, but the school's rules prohibit students from using magic within its premises. This rule resulted from some students being unable to control their magical energies and spells fully. And once a spell isn't handled correctly, it can have a ridiculous, often disastrous result. For example, a young girl in one of the classes had once used her magic to ward off a persistent fly; unfortunately, she said the spell wrongly, and it backfired, turning the fly into a tree. The tree grew so big that its roots spread all over the school, knocking down walls and pushing people aside. It grew so tall that it went through the roof, costing the school a lot in repairs. Following the incident, coupled with some other similar incidents, the use of magic has been limited to Magic classes where the art is taught. It is also permitted for the mild raising of objects and teleportation outside the school building.

Aiden enters the class only to find it in session. He peers through the room full of students standing side by side in search of his two friends. Finally, he spots them after a brief but thorough search. It takes a while to get their attention but seeing the thickness and tightness of the students sandwiching him; they knew it'd only take a miracle for them to be together. The students wouldn't want to move if they beckoned, and this was something they weren't ready to handle, so they stayed put. Aiden, however, manages to get to them.

"Hey," he greets as he stands between them

"You are late," Himmel says with a smirk

"I know. I hope I haven't missed anything." Aiden asks, squinting as he turns his head around.

"Not much. Two sets have fought already, and they are getting ready for the next round." Meeryn answered. "Wait, how were you even able to get through all those people?" she asks in amusement.

"Well, I pushed them aside," Aiden answers casually.

Meeryn and Himmel look at him in disbelief. They both ponder how he could push the students, and nothing happened. It also makes them question their decision to stay instead of joining him where he was. Perhaps they'd have been able to do the same.

"Really?" Meeryn asks with astonishment in her eyes.

"No, I didn't," Aiden says, laughing. "How could I? They all looked mean. Since I couldn't ask them for permission, I swarm through them instead," he adds.

"It's the game," Himmel says faintly.

"What?" Aiden and Meeryn ask in unison.

"It's the game. It changes you, me, them, everyone in here. They all want to win, so they become hard-spirited," Himmel says with folded arms and eyes, looking intently into the crowd as though waiting for something to happen.

"Yeah, I guess so. This is one of the moments some of us get to show just how good we are, so I get why they would be like this," Aiden adds, almost not concerned about the state of the moment.

Himmel nods his head in agreement with Aiden's words. He takes a side look at Aiden on his left, and he says, "You haven't changed your clothes yet?"

Aiden's eyes darts to his clothes almost immediately, "Oh, I almost forgot," and in the blink of an eye, his whole outfit changes into his team's practice outfit - a blue cotton shirt, thick red pants, and black boots. Although the practice uniforms are the same, they differ in color from one team to another, and it is mandatory for every student to wear their team's outfit during the fight practice. Himmel's team wears yellow shirts with white pants, while Meeryn's team wears orange shirts with black pants. All teams wear black boots.

"There!" he exclaims, looking at his practice outfit, "Oh, I have something to tell you both," Aiden adds with a smile.

"What is it?" They ask

"It's about ---"

"And the next round is between Fidemoore and Aiden," a voice interrupts from the speakers.

"What?" Aiden yells in shock.

"Well, won't you go?" Himmel asks.

"I will. I just want to let you know that I'm going for the ---"

"Aiden, we don't have all day," one of the teachers standing close by tells him.

Aiden walks towards the ring and then turns back to his friends, "I'm going for the Institute's tryout with you guys," he says loud enough for them to hear.

Meeryn and Himmel's faces brighten up as they give each other a surprised look, wondering what changed his mind.

CHAPTER 6

HIDDEN POWER

Chapter Six

Hidden Power

At the beginning of the senior year, students are divided into teams for their fight practice class. A student from one team has to fight a student from another, and whoever wins gets the point. Eventually, the point from each team member is accumulated to determine the team's overall point. The team with the highest points wins.

Aiden walks into the ring, a square-shaped platform with pillars on all four sides. These stone pillars produce a shield that blocks off any magical attack an opponent in the ring dodges, preventing it from hitting the spectators outside. The platform is slightly elevated to give the spectators a better view. Aiden's opponent is a boy named Fidemoore, a level 10 sorcerer from Lildephia. He was born to a merchant father and a mother who cleans houses for the nobles in Cremindale (now part of Belbourgh). Due to his background, he is always resolved to win his fights, and because of this, he studies hard, practices his magic assiduously, and tries to learn as many spells as possible. His hard work has gotten him to the 10th level as a sorcerer and a strong contender. Fidemoore has grey eyes, dark but short hair, slightly pale skin, and a full oval face. He has a fit body that is neither muscular nor thin. He's athletic too, so he participates in sports. However, he doesn't like Aiden that much because he feels Aiden is getting certain privileges based on his good looks. Aiden is good-looking, with a face so radiant and hair so lustrous that he'd pass for a fairy from Winxforte, but that isn't the case. Aiden has more magical energy and potential than twenty people combined, including Fidemoore.

"Hey, if you are going, then you better win this," Himmel screams through the chattering crowd, getting Aiden's attention.

"Pfft, sure I will," Aiden says, believing in his ability since it isn't the first time he is fighting Fidemoore.

Due to the subtle envy that Fidemoore has for Aiden, he has approached him for a duel multiple times just to see who's stronger. Aiden refused every time he did, including when he tried to use words to get to him. This went on for a while until one day when Fidemoore used Meeryn as his bait. He'd seen Aiden and Meeryn together, so he walked up to them and asked Aiden for a duel, and as the last time, Aiden refused.

Fidemoore wouldn't let it be, so he cast a spell on Meeryn. He merged the unsuspecting girl with a nearby tree and said to Aiden, "*The only way I will let her go is if you fight me. If you don't, she remains there.*" Aiden was perplexed as neither he nor Meeryn knew how to reverse the spell. However, he knew he had no choice but to accept Fidemoore's challenge.

He was in a rage when the fight began, so he fired rays of repulsive light at Fidemoore, which sent him flying through the air, and on his back. Immediately, he cast another spell with his fingers to strap Fidemoore to the ground with roots shooting out of the ground to hold him in place. Unable to move, Fidemoore opted for words to cast a spell to regain his freedom, but Aiden quickly ran one of the roots over his mouth, stopping him from saying anything.

Finally, when he saw he was approaching defeat, he yielded to Aiden's order to let Meeryn out of the tree. He cast the reverse spell, and she came out unharmed. Meeryn walked over to Fidemoore and gave him a hard slap across his face. Aiden shakes his head as he jerks back to the present moment. He smiles at Fidemoore, but he doesn't seem to be in the mood to return it. Instead, he gives Aiden a contemptuous gaze. They are about to fight again, this time in front of everyone, and he sees it as his shot to redeem himself his their last encounter.

"Loosen up, Fidemoore. It's just a school game," Aiden starts, "Let's not blow it out of proportion," he adds.

"If blowing it out of proportion means blowing you away, then I'll be more than glad to do so," Fidemoore says in disgust.

With a sigh, Aiden replies, "If that's the way you want it, we will do it your way then."

"The third round is about to start. Fighters, take your position," the voice from the speaker notifies them.

Aiden and Fidemoore walk a few inches toward each other as they take their stance, ready for the fight. The pillars come alive with a fiery glow as the top of each pillar blows up with fire coming out of it. The shield manifests itself, covering the fighters within the ring.

"You all know the rules, the first person to be thrown out of the ring wins. Now, begin!" says the same voice, followed by a dong from a bell.

Fidemoore moves in swiftly, attacking with a rope-like light material he created. He wraps it around Aiden's leg, pulling him across the floor of the fighting ring. It's his first attempt at throwing Aiden out of there, and it seems to be working. Sensing defeat, Aiden opens a portal a few inches from the shield and goes through it. He takes everyone by surprise as he reappears shortly in front of Fidemoore. He recreates Fidemoore's initial trick and throws him off balance, down to the floor.

Recalling the event from the last time, Fidemoore gets up quickly but is pushed back to the ground by Aiden's swirling wind. He sees a slash of energy coming toward him as he attempts to stand, so he quickly casts a spell that dispels the energy. He uses that opportunity to stand fully and cast another spell. The spell creates several portals around Aiden, leaving both Aiden and the crowd wondering what would come out of them. In a heartbeat, rope-like materials spring out of these portals and take hold of Aiden, making it difficult for him to move.

Fidemoore, seeing that Aiden cannot move, mutters, "*I have got you now, you proud bastard,*" and runs towards him to give him the final blow. Aiden sees Fidemoore running toward him, and he soon realizes he may lose. He's trying to think of what to do to break free, but he can't come up with anything. He shuts his eyes as Fidemoore is about to give him a double flying kick from the air, but suddenly, there's a release of massive bursts of energy from his body. It sends Fidemoore and the students standing close to the ring flying back. The crowd cheers as he manages to break free with that act. He goes for Fidemoore in one final attack, bringing him up with his levitation powers. Satisfied with the height, he sends a massive energy blast at his opponent, causing him to fly out of the ring and making him the winner.

"Wow! That was a close one," he says with relief.

Everywhere goes silent for a while, as students, his friends, and Fidemoore stare at him with bewilderment, he looks around to see everyone looking at him, and he is worried. Soon, Himmel starts clapping, followed by Meeryn, and in a matter of seconds, there is a roaring sound of applause for Aiden's win and show of power during the fight. He starts to feel relieved and soon screams to the crowd in excitement. Finally, he walks out of the ring to his cheering friends while Fidemoore, on the other hand, storms out of the class angrily for losing to Aiden once again.

"Whoa, what did you do back there with the energy?" Himmel asks Aiden with peering eyes.

"I don't know. It just happened," Aiden answers truthfully.

"So, it wasn't a spell that you cast?" Meeryn asked.

"No, it wasn't," Aiden replies

"Then, what was it?!" Meeryn and Himmel chorus.

"I don't know. I guess it just happened because I was scared I would lose to Fidemoore," Aiden tells his friends.

"So, you released an energy that blew us away because you were scared you would lose?" Himmel asks rhetorically.

Aiden shrugs his shoulders at Himmel.

"Hey, your right arm is glowing," Meeryn says, pointing to Aiden's right arm.

Both Aiden and Himmel look at the arm and see that it's indeed glowing, through a mark Aiden thinks he got from an injury he had when he was younger. The mark from his elbow and around his arm is now emitting a bright yellow light. Aiden can't seem to come up with any reason the mark is emitting the light, but after a few minutes, it stops.

"Okay, that was weird. When did such start?" Meeryn asks Aiden with concern.

"I don't know," he replies in a low tone.

"You get creepier by the day. First, energy shoots out of your body, and now, this! What else will happen? Will your eyes turn blue too?" Himmel blurts out in sarcasm.

"Yes," Aiden answers, retuning the sarcastic tone. However, he keeps staring at the mark on his arm, unsure of what is happening.

CHAPTER 7

MAGIC INSTITUTE TRYOUTS

It's the day fixed for the tryout, and everyone is ecstatic as they prepare for the exercise. As this is a tryout where since the participants will use magical spells, they are brushing up on their skills, practicing, and getting themselves pumped up for it. The Institute will test each candidate's endurance, intelligence, speed level, and magical energy intensity through the exercise. The stronger your magic, the higher chance your chances of being selected.

Himmel and Meeryn are outside Aiden's house practicing while they wait for him to get ready. Himmel casts a spell that pulls boulders out from the ground and instructs Meeryn to hold them up for as long as she can, even if her legs want to give up on her.

"What if I exhaust myself before the tryouts?" Meeryn asks him in worry

"Don't worry; I have something that'd replenish your energy. It'll be as though you haven't done anything today." Himmel boasts as he assures her

Meeryn thinks it through for a moment before she finally agrees. She casts a spell that raises the boulder above the height of Aiden's parents' house and holds them there. She does well for about three minutes before she starts to shake. By the fifth minute, her hand starts to fail her, making it difficult to hold up the boulders with them. Nearly exhausted, she falls to the ground but still has her hand up to hold the boulders. This only goes on for another two minutes before she releases the boulders.

"I give up, Himmel," she screams.

Aiden walks through the door to join them outside as if on cue.

"Whoa, what's going on here?" he asks, seeing Meeryn's exhausted body at the corner of the compound.

"We are practicing," Himmel replies, helping Meeryn up.

"Yes, we are practicing," Meeryn repeats, trying to catch her breath.

"Okay... but isn't that going to exhaust you before the tryout?" Aiden asks, visibly concerned.

"You don't have to worry, we still have some time, and I have something that'd put her in tip-top shape in no time," Himmel says, reassuring them as he brings out a small bottle from his shirt pocket,

"This will give Meeryn back her energy," he says, holding up the bottle with purple mix liquid.

He gives it to Meeryn, who takes it without saying anything. Soon, the portion starts to kick in, and she begins to regain strength.

"Huh... this does work," she says, smiling at Himmel.

Both Aiden and Himmel smile at Meeryn

"We should leave now if we don't want to be late." Aiden urges them.

Aiden's mother sees them preparing to leave and runs out of the house to wish them success. The trio turns around for the blessings.

"Thank you, ma," they chorus before bidding her farewell.

***

There are a lot of people at the venue for the exercise. One can tell from their looks that they are seemingly confident in their abilities and are ready to give their best. The institute has designed its tryout exercise in such a way that everybody can participate, and if you meet the standard, you'll get picked. Some of the participants are with their older siblings who have made it into the institute and are officers in some of the corps. The experienced officers share their knowledge as they help their younger siblings and friends practice. Aiden and his friends are amazed by it, wishing they were that lucky.

The main event begins, and corps officers are out to coordinate the participants. The officers ask all the participants to gather in one place as they divide them into six groups, consisting of twenty people per group. Anyone who fulfills the requirement from any of the groups will be picked. Unlike school fight practice, no points will be awarded to any group; instead, it'd just be a selection of preferred candidates. Also, each group gets only one trial.

The tests are designed in such a way that when a participant is unable to complete a specific test and is about to be crushed, in the event of a death-threatening test, a corps officer will come in to get that person out or stop whatever is about to hit or kill the person. This process is adopted to choose the strongest participants who they believe are those that can complete their difficult test. Aiden, Himmel, and Meeryn are in the same group, which happens to be the last group to take the exercise.

The first five groups take the exercise, and the candidates that stand out from each group are selected. There was jubilation, as well as cries, as the selection was ongoing.

The groups had people with impressive skills. Some were so strong that they pulverized boulders to dust in one strike, some so smart that they knew when an attack was an illusion and knew the right spell to break out of it. Some others were so fast that they could cast multiple spells in seconds. Not just ordinarily spells but spells that'd take some sorcerers minutes to cast completely.

An exciting part of the tryouts was the exercise given to a girl with yellow eyes and dark skin. She was to avoid four attacks – a charging Godenhorg, flying arrows, a fire blast from one of the officers in the corps, and a metal cube as big as a house coming down on her from above. She had to avoid all four attacks simultaneously and at short range. The purpose of the exercise was to test how fast she would react.

Everyone was afraid she couldn't do it. Still, somehow, she was able to put the Godenhorg in a cage of fire, halt the flying arrows in the air, pull up a stone wall to block the fire from the officer, and create a portal big enough for the metal cube above her to pass through and land somewhere else. Her speed in casting spells was highly remarkable, and even though she came third in the group, she was chosen first before the others.

Having witnessed all these feats, the participants in the last group begins to panic, second-guessing their chances of winning. Aiden and his friends were mostly quiet throughout the other groups' tryouts and didn't say much to each other. They were thinking of what they'd do in there, the spells to cast, the moves to showcase, their speed level, etc. They kept wondering how they could measure up to some of the participants in their group.

Aiden looks around to observe the remaining seventeen people in their group, only to see most of them looking very tough as if to show that they're ready for whatever would be thrown at them. However, some look calm and expressionless. As they make their way to the testing ground big enough to take over a hundred people, someone within the group interrupts whatever thought is running through their mind as he makes way for the entrance. As he runs, he mutters, "*I can't do this. I can't do this.*"

The crowd burst into laughter as they watch the young man running away. At that moment, a voice yells, "You are only as strong as your will. *You will fail this tryout if you don't believe in yourself.*"

In a short time, normalcy is restored as the candidates in the last group receive their task. The instructor asks Meeryn to use levitation to move three big metal cubes, weighing as much as six houses, through four hoops about ten feet apart. Himmel's task is to kill forty bats without falling to the ground. The bats are as big as a griffon, and he has to complete it in five minutes. Aiden's task is to fight a giant magical beast. The beast is bigger than a Godenhorg, making the ground quake when it walks. This beast isn't easy to kill, and only a strong sorcerer will be capable of killing it.

Himmel starts his task, trying to kill the bats as fast as he can, but he doesn't seem to be having it easy as the bats are equally very fast in the air. They charge at him with overwhelming speed. He has to run and jump multiple to evade their sharp teeth. As he does this, he gets a strike or two, helping him slice some of the bats into two or severing their heads. Killing the bats is difficult, but Himmel is visibly doing well.

Meeryn, on the other hand, is moving the metal cube through the hoops, but she finds it difficult to hold them up. Due to their weight, holding them will be hard for someone without endurance, yet she tries to push on. At this point, she wishes to have some more of Himmel's portion.

The beast confronts Aiden, and he can't help but wonder why an institute such as the Earlmond Magic Institute would be making participants fight a beast for tryouts. While he's still thinking, the giant beast launches an attack on him with one of its legs. Aiden sees it and quickly goes out of the way. The beast follows him for another attack, making him increase his pace. As he runs around, he tries to think of what to do. While running, he turns back and sends an energy blast at the beast, but it doesn't seem to affect it; instead, it keeps running towards him. It gets to Aiden and pushes him down, brushing the ground as he falls. Soon, the beast pounces on Aiden, raising dust into the air. The other participants are scared for him. Meeryn loses concentration as she sees her friend being attacked by the beast. She pauses out of fear making the metal cubes slightly fall from the air. She brings them back up again, albeit with great difficulty. An officer attempts to assist Aiden, but one of the generals stops him.

The dust clears, and everyone sees Aiden in a shield he created to protect himself from the beast's jaws, but this doesn't stop the beast. Instead, it hits the shield repeatedly, biting and stomping on it with its weight, trying to break it. As the shield starts to crack, Aiden realizes that the longer he stays there, the slimmer his chances of winning. He quickly conjures multiple portals around the beast, and by crossing his hands, huge bursts of fire come rushing out of the portals onto the beast. The fire burst is so overwhelming that it moves the beast away, giving Aiden time to cancel the shield spell. The beast sees him as he gets up and charges toward him again. It tries to pounce on Aiden again, but he's quick to teleport to its back. The beast takes him unaware as it wraps its tail around his legs, continuously tossing him around on the ground. Hurt by it, Aiden casts a spell that conjures up swords made of energy and sends them into the beast at a speed it couldn't counter. The blades dive deep into the beast and kill it. At the end of the group's exercise, Aiden and Himmel are among the most preferred candidates from their group. Unfortunately, Meeryn couldn't make it.

"You could try out again in the next five years," Aiden says to her.

"Orientation and training start in two days," the officers announced as they dismissed the candidates.

Himmel and Aiden spend their journey home consoling and cheering Meeryn up.

CHAPTER 8

EARLMOND MAGIC INSTITUTE

The Earlmond Magic Institute is buzzing with people as it welcomes the recruit. Himmel and Aiden arrive at the premises with the other students and are fascinated as they walk through. Out of excitement, Himmel begins to jump around as he sings praises of the Institute. He finds everything about the place exciting, especially the fact that it is in the sky. The Institute organized the most amazing means of transportation the boys have ever seen. All the successful candidates were gathered in a place waiting for further instructions, after which a chariot propelled by four flying wings arrived and flew them all to the Institute.

As Aiden and Himmel are still taking in the grandeur of the place, a voice belonging to an officer screams through their moment of wonder, disrupting their thoughts. They turn toward the man to get a better view of him and listen to what he has to say.

"Welcome to the Earlmond Magic institute. As you may already know, the Institute is responsible for protecting and safeguarding the kingdoms from evil magical beasts, extremely powerful but evil sorcerers and sorceresses, magical disturbances in the land, and training the kingdom's armies. This training is to prepare you for war and equip you with all you need to know about protecting all kingdoms. We are an independent and elite force of warriors with no allegiance to any kingdom. We only serve to protect all kingdoms from threats too difficult to handle," the officer starts.

He spells out the routine and rules of the Institute as he continues the orientation. Finally, he rounds off by assigning the recruits to officers who'd lead them to their respective rooms.

"Training starts tomorrow, so get as much rest as possible. Good luck, everyone!"

The man walks off the stage as the students start walking toward their assigned officers. Aiden and Himmel bid each other farewell as they part ways. Although both boys had planned to stay together, they were assigned to different rooms.

It takes Aiden a few minutes to get to his room. He takes a deep breath before walking through the door. He stops midway as he notices someone who he perceives to be his roommate hanging in the air.

"Hey! I'm Aiden," he says, introducing himself.

"Hello, Aiden. I'm Dayan. Nice to meet you," the floating boy says as he lands a few meters away from Aiden. He attempts to help Aiden with his bags, but he politely declines as he walks into the room. Aiden starts unpacking as Dayan starts small talks.

"You know, I wish we could all fly without having to cast any spell. So that flying becomes natural to us like it is with the birds," Dayan says dryly.

"Yes, I wish so myself," Aiden replies.

Soon, the conversation between Aiden and Dayan shifts from wishes to other things.

They talk about their families, hobbies, inspiration to join the Institute, task at the tryouts, life back home, and many other things. Aiden is exhausted from unpacking, so he sits on his bed for a moment, still listening to Dayan talk.

"Do you have a girlfriend at home?" Dayan asks him.

"Not really. But I do have a friend whom I've known since I was nine. She would have been here too but didn't make it through the tryout," Aiden replies, laying on his bed and staring into the ceiling.

"Oh, that's terrible," Dayan says, crossing his legs in the air.

"Yeah, it is," Aiden responds, shutting his eyes.

***

The following day, the students gather in an open field, standing in a fine military pattern of rows and columns. The students are waiting anxiously to be assigned to their Corps. The process is based on the unique power feats they displayed during the tryouts. The students aspire to join the highest Corps, the Fremin Magix Corps, to become powerful magic users.

The wait finally comes to an end when an officer climbs the stage. Silence envelopes the field as the students listen to the officer call out their names and their respective Corps from a scroll. There is a mixture of excitement and sadness as the students hear their names. The students who make it to the Fremin Magix Corps are jumping around in joy, while the ones who didn't are carrying are wearing sad faces. Even though many of them are dismayed by the turnout of the event, they are consoled by the fact that the Institute thought they were good enough to accept them.

Himmel is one of the students who didn't make it into Fremin Magix Corps. Disappointment and anger wash through him as he hears his name. He stands still for a moment, letting memories from the tryout flash through his mind. He clenches his fist as he tries to grasp his head around the whole event. "*I killed forty-four bats within my stipulated time frame, so what went wrong?*" He thinks to himself. He had resumed the previous day feeling that he stood a good chance at making it to the highest Corps but here he is with dashing hopes of ever becoming a sorcerer worth contending with. He walks over to the section assigned to the Orion Corps, still trying to figure it out.

"Can you please confirm that I'm actually supposed to be here?" He asks the officer in charge of coordinating the members of the Corps.

"There is no mistake, young man," the officer replies dismissively.

Himmel's disappointment doubles as he hears Aiden being assigned to the highest

Corps. Aiden was indifferent about the whole process right from the beginning, and he didn't think he did well at the tryouts, so it was a miracle that he was among the successful candidates and, now, a member of the Fregmin Magix Corps. Himmel looks back, and his eyes meet Aiden's. He gives him an awkward half-smile before looking away. Aiden feels bad for his friend, but there's nothing either of them can do to change anything. He returns his attention to the officer only to hear Dayan's name and his assigned Corps. He sighs in relief, knowing he wouldn't be going through the training at Fregmin Magix Corps alone.

Finally, the officer calls out all the names and then gives the students, especially friends who didn't make it to the same Corps, a few minutes to say their parting words.

Every Corps in the Institute has its designated camp, so members from different Corps don't see each other unless there's an emergency. The first Corps stay in one section of the floating superstructure, giving them an exclusive area for their training. The second, third, and fourth Corps stay together in another section of the superstructure.

"I guess we will be seeing each other next time, then," Aiden starts, unsure of what to say.

"Yes, it's quite unfair, but I'm already here, so I might as well just go with it," Himmel replies as he turns to leave.

"Hey, take care of yourself, okay?"

"Of course, I will. I am Himmel Daegon,"

They hug each other briefly before going off to their respective corps building.

CHAPTER 9

TIANA VOSS

Today is the first day of the training, and the students are excited about it. They've been in the Institute for five days, and every moment has been blissful. Aiden and his roommate, Dayan, have spent all morning talking about the training. They put final touches on their outfits as they step out of their room. A voice runs through the building revealing the venue for the training. The students whisper in anticipation until they hear the last part of the announcement.

"How are we supposed to get there in one minute?" one of the boys cries

Without waiting for answers, the students take to their heels, running towards the training venue. After running a few meters, they eventually arrive at the venue. The officers at the entrance decide to pardon the latecomers since it's the first training. However, they give a stern warning against a reoccurrence.

"Oh, High Father, I think I need to tour this place. I need to be familiar with all the training grounds, so I won't have to run next time," Dayan says, holding his knees and out of breath.

"You can say that again," Aiden says with a heaving chest.

"Hello, boys and girls! Welcome to the Fremin Magix Corps. I'll need you all to stand erect and pay attention!" a female voice calls out, interrupting the indistinct chatters among the students who are still trying to catch their breaths.

The students slowly turn around, gazing at the woman and wondering what she'd say or do next.

"Good!" she says, walking in the air, "I know you all are glad to be here. Most of you have always dreamt of being part of this corps, which is good. Although, you wouldn't have been here if not for your quick thinking, strength, and raw magic energy, which you demonstrated during the tryout. I must say, I was impressed, and I hope you all continue to impress me." She pauses to look around briefly

"I will be your instructor for most of your training routines, which means you'd get to see me a lot. A whole lot. So, whatever you do, keep up the confidence level and put your all into this training. The Fremin Magix Corps isn't for weak sorcerers and sorceresses, do you understand?" she asks, with a tone loud enough for everyone in the room to hear.

"Yes!" the students reply.

"Repeat after me; the Fremin Magix Corps isn't for weak sorcerers and sorceresses," she screams again.

"The Fremin Magix Corps isn't for weak sorcerers and sorceresses," the students echo.

Meanwhile, Aiden's focus is elsewhere. He can't seem to take his eyes off the instructor. He tries a couple of times but still finds himself giving her the 'look.' He watches the way she walks in the air, moving from one point to another, the way she flips her hair, the way she's addressing them, everything about her just seems to catch his fancy. Aiden can't help but wonder how many noble, powerful, and influential men in all five kingdoms have tried to woo her. He assesses her facial features again, smiling to himself. He's trying to come up with ideas to get her attention so he'd profess his feelings for her when someone accidentally hits him, bringing him back to reality.

"Alright! Your first training will be moving a training obstacle course. You all would have to run through it, dodging all its obstacles. Remember, use your head while on it. The test is to assess individual smartness. Okay, get ready," she tells them.

Moments later, she teleports with all the students to the area where the training obstacle course is kept. Unfortunately, most of the students fall to the ground as they land. The teleportation was sudden and unexpected.

"I told you all to get ready, didn't I?" she asks with a smile.

The students do not bother to answer. Instead, they help those on the floor back to their feet while waiting for further instructions.

"I almost forgot to mention. My name is Tiana, Tiana Voss, and I'd like you all to start running! Now!" she commands, screaming out her last statement.

The students barely have time to grasp the revelation before starting the training. Most of the students find it hard to believe their instructor is the revered and powerful sorceress, Tiana Voss.

After about three hours of training, the students are exhausted and begin to find it difficult to pass the course. When the instructor notices their poor performance, she dismisses them. They go to their rooms to freshen up before heading to the cafeteria for food.

"Wow, that Tiana lady is something else, isn't she?" Aiden asks, almost merging his words with his breath as he falls to his bed

"Yeah, she is. She almost killed us," Dayan says, rubbing his left shoulder in pain.

"But, we aren't dead," Aiden teases.

"If we keep going at this rate, we might soon be," Dayan hisses

"Oh, calm down, Dayan, we will be alright," Aiden says, laughing at his roommate

"I hope so,"

"Also, don't you think our instructor, Tiana, is cool? I mean, the way she talks, moves, and runs, is all very cool."

"I know that kind of talk, Aiden. And yes, she's cool, but she's way out of your league," Dayan says truthfully.

"Why? Because she's our instructor and a general?"

"Yes, and—"

"...because she's more skillful than me, more powerful, and much older?"

"Yes, that too, but—"

"...because she's —"

"Stop interrupting, Aiden! I'm trying to tell you something!" Dayan blurts out

Both boys remain quiet for a few minutes as if thinking of what next to say. Then, finally, Aiden breaks the silence with his question.

"What is it?" he asks, looking intently at Dayan, who's now lying on his bed.

Dayan takes a deep breath before answering. "She's from a house of nobles. Her name isn't Tiana Voss by accident. She's the daughter of Lord Voss Gridael, the right-hand man to the king of Belbourgh. He's the man who planned all the attacks and strategies used by the Belbourgh army to take Cremindale. It is also known that women from noble houses can't be with men who aren't nobles themselves. So, you can't be with her, as she wouldn't even want to be with you."

"Whoa, that's a lot," Aiden says with a sad voice.

"That's what I was trying to tell you, but you kept on—"

"Whatever it may be, I'll still try and get to her, no matter what!" Aiden says, cutting Dayan short for the umpteenth time.

Annoyed by Aiden's behavior, Dayan remains silent. He turns over to face the wall and soon drifts into sleep. Aiden joins in, forgetting they're supposed to be at the cafeteria for lunch.

***

The following weeks have Aiden falling even deeper for Tiana. He has never been this way with other girls and never thought about other girls the way he thinks of Tiana, even Meeryn, who was vocal about her feelings for him. He doesn't even know why he's suddenly drawn to Tiana. The more he sees her, the more he's conscious of her presence and how he feels about her. Due to his flirtatious behavior towards her, she'd often make him do double the exercise others did. Instead of getting sad or angry, Aiden will gladly take on the task just to impress her.

Dayan was right about her being out of his league, but he just couldn't get her out of his head. He has had crushes and admiration for other maidens, but it is never that deep. His feelings for Tiana are different and more concrete. It makes him anxious anytime he thinks of her, sees her, or even hears her voice. Everything about her excites him, reinforcing his decision to tell her how he feels.

CHAPTER 10

CONFESSIONS

It's another training session, and everyone is at the training ground, waiting for the instructor. It's been over a month since the training commenced, and they moved into the Fremin Magix Corps quarters. Most students are now familiar with the building, even though they still teleport around the premises to avoid unnecessary delay. After a short time of waiting, a portal opens, revealing their instructor. Tiana joins the students beaming with smiles. She looks around, confirming looks that all students are present. She gives Aiden a contemptuous sneer as their eyes lock for a few seconds. He gives her a full smile, not minding her sneer. It's been a month of nurturing his feelings, and he's yet to tell her how he feels about her. He had different experiences with women, but none involved anxiety. He could easily walk to any girl to profess his feelings and get positive feedback, but this time, he kept stalling.

"It's good that you are all here. I wouldn't want anybody to miss this special training. Today, we'll be using spells in defense," Tiana tells her students.

"Finally, some action..."

"Yeah!" "Now, I get to show my skills..."

"This is amazing,"

"Enough!" Tiana yells, breaking the rising chatter in the arena.

"I know most of you are happy that you'll finally get to use your combat magic to show some fighting skills, and that's good, but if you don't impress me, you will repeat it until I am satisfied," she says, stretching her last word as the hovers above the students.

"Do you all understand that?"

"Yes, ma!" the excited students chorus.

"Alright, divide yourselves into groups of twos and start practicing," she instructs

The students walk around looking for the perfect partner to pair with. Aiden turns down several requests, mostly from girls, until he finds Dayan at a corner. Soon, everyone is paired up in twos, ready to start fighting.

"Alright, begin!" Tiana orders.

The students launch their attack, displaying their skills in different dimensions.

"Dayan, I have finally made up my mind to tell her how I feel," Aiden tells his partner, Dayan.

“Who? Our instructor?” Dayan asks.

“Uh-huh,” he replies, smiling.

“I have told you this, Aiden, it won’t work. She has been hard on you these past few weeks, don’t you see it?” Dayan asks with visible annoyance

“I do. I have this feeling she knows I like her, but she’s waiting for me to spill it,”

“So, you want to tell her so that she can reaffirm her thoughts about you?”

“It’s worth a shot, right?”

“No! It’s a bad idea; we know where this will lead if you do. See, I might even get caught up in it,” Dayan points out.

“No, you won’t,” Aiden says convincingly.

Dayan slips in the middle of casting a spell, causing him to lose control. This causes his hands to release a powerful blast of energy that cuts through the students.

As the energy blast flies through, the students quickly get out of the way to avoid a hit. This goes on for a few seconds until Aiden sees the energy blast approaching an unsuspecting Tiana. He teleports in front of her in an instant, conjuring a red shield with symbols all over it. The blast hits the shield at the exact moment he covers Tiana.

"Are you okay?" he asks her.

Tiana doesn't answer, only rolling her eyes at him. Her eyes widen as she sees the shield in front of her.

"Where did you learn to conjure up this shield?" Tiana asks, returning her gaze to him.

"Huh, this? I learned it at the corps' library three days ago. The book said the shield protects you from energy attacks and absorbs the energy into it, allowing you to shoot it back with even greater force. I have no idea why this came up in my head," Aiden answers, rubbing his head.

Tiana's stern face loosens as she stares at Aiden with admiration and awe. She's wondering how someone can maintain the DYO shield for that long. Aiden stares back at her blue eyes, thinking of the next thing to say to her. He doesn't even have an idea of what to do next. They seem lost as they draw even deeper into each other's gaze, leaving behind the murmuring students. After a few minutes of staying in that position, Tiana gets the feeling that she's not alone in the room and soon comes back to her senses. She looks around to catch the questioning looks of her students, who are visibly gossiping about the incident.

"Get back in line. I am more than capable of handling any situation, so keep your saving to yourself." Tiana yells at him, shattering the shield in anger.

"Okay, I will go now," Aiden says, returning to Dayan.

"It wouldn't hurt you to say 'thank you,' at least," he mutters. Dayan gives him a smirk.

Tiana becomes embarrassed from seeing the students chuckle as they reminisce on the brief tension between her and Aiden. She storms out of the training ground and teleports a few feet from the entrance with a strong force that sends wind echoes throughout the arena, signifying her power.

"Can you see what you've done? She's upset, and we are so going to die from this," Dayan says, lamenting.

"Yes," Aiden replies, staring at the entrance, considering if he should go after her or not.

"Yes?" Dayan asks in confusion.

Aiden looks away, paying him no attention.

***

Tiana enters her quarters briskly. She shuts the door behind her and leans on it for a moment, sighing repeatedly. Then, when she feels better, she walks over to a chair in one corner of the room. She waves her hand at the bowl of fruits on a table at the entrance as she sinks into the chair. She makes a cup of juice out of the fruits, and it comes to her. She takes a gulp and sets the cup on the stool next to her.

"Who does that Aiden boy think he is? Does he think a general like me can't handle herself?" she says to herself.

As she goes over the episode with Aiden, she cannot help but acknowledge that the young man is getting through her walls. She has shrugged off the thought of him in her several times, but anytime he comes up, she'd have a swirling feeling. This feeling often makes her a bit dizzy. Constantly increasing his task is her way of reminding herself that she's older and in no way at the same level as him. Besides, it's forbidden in any of the five kingdoms for a girl from a noble home to marry someone outside of nobility.

Tiana's face changes as a tender smile curls on her lips. She stares into the ceiling, looking at nothing in particular. She jerks back to reality when she hears a knock on her door.

"Who is it?" she asks authoritatively.

"Open up and see for yourself," the voice on the other side of the door answers.

The thick masculine voice sounds like it belongs to an older person; hence, Tiana becomes suspicious. She conjures a shield as she slowly gets up from her seat. She stealthily makes her way to the door, putting the shield up to her face with her left hand. The door flies open, sending Tiana back when she extends her hand to the knob. She attempts to attack but stops in her track as she recognizes the person in front of her. Immediately, she falls to her knees.

"Greetings, father! My apologies," she says, facing down.

"It's alright, Tiana. Rise," the man replies.

"Thank you, father,"

"Hmm,"

"What brings you here today?" She asks as she ushers him in.

"I came to see my best daughter, or can't I come to see you again?" He asks with a smirk.

Tiana's face brightens upon hearing her father's words

"Of course, father, you can," she answers with a beaming smile

"Good. So, how are you doing?"

"I am doing very well. I have these students I'm teaching now, and they are all very promising. There's even this boy who doesn't—" she rambles.

"How's the plan going?" Lord Gridael cuts in, obviously uninterested in his daughter's tales.

Tiana's face falls when she realizes her father didn't come to see her because he cares or wants to know how she's doing. He came for business.

"I see," she says, swallowing a lump in her throat, "Well, the plan is going quite well, father. I am very close to cracking the spells. Very soon, you and the king will have what you want," she adds, sternly.

"Do not forget the reason you are here. You have been trained all these years so that you can help our kingdom fight her enemies. So, keep getting stronger and carry out all your assignment as instructed. But, unfortunately, the others we assigned aren't progressing as much as we want, leaving just you in the grand scheme, and for that, I am proud of you, my daughter. I am proud that you follow your orders well, and I am proud you killed that king. You didn't only make me proud, you made your king proud as well," Lord Gridael says as he fixes his gaze on his daughter.

Tiana raises her head to meet his gaze, her expression shifting from a serious to a warm look. She's speechless, and at the same time, she wants to cry and hug her father, saying "thank you," but isn't sure if he would like it. Lord Gridael has never shown his emotional side to Tiana or her siblings, which always bothers her. Her silent wish has always been for her father to treat her more like a child than a soldier.

"Thank you, father," she says regardless, standing to her feet.

A knock comes through the door, and Tiana waves her hand over it, revealing the person on the other side to her and her father. She knows who the guest is, and before she could say anything to her father, he vanishes. She makes a mirror-like object appear before her, looking at her reflection as she clenches her fist. The person at the door knocks again for the umpteenth time, forcing Tiana to speak.

"Come in," she says dryly.

Aiden comes through the door and walks until he's standing a few meters from where Tiana is sitting. She gestures for him to sit adjacent to her, and he complies.

"Hello, general, I hope I am not disturbing," Aiden asks

"No, you are not. What is it?" she asks him, picking up her cup of fruit juice.

"Nothing, I just came to see if you're doing okay,"

Tiana gives him a prying look.

Aiden understands the look and quickly adds, "I know you are doing okay; it's just that I came to explain what happened back there. See, I didn't mean to be the hero or anything. I know you could've easily stopped that blast with your bare hands, maybe your fingers even. I didn't know what came over me that made me step in for you,"

"It's alright. It's nice to have a guy save a girl now and then. I do the saving most times," she says, laughing, "...and killing," she adds, lowering her face in sadness.

"I know your father must be proud of you,"

"Yeah, my father, he sure is," she says, sounding dejected.

"What's wrong, general?" Aiden asks, noticing the change in her voice

"It's nothing really. It's just that my father isn't one to treat his children with so much love. His definition of love is allegiance to the kingdom and doing things he wants you to do. He pushed most of us, his children, to train and train, harnessing and honing our magical powers to become experts. He would often use us to achieve his or the king's aim. We expect that he'd show us some form of love whenever we complete a task, but that doesn't seem to be something he sees. He only cares about pleasing the king and getting more money from his position. Position and power are all he seeks, and it irritates me, yet, whenever he gives an order, I always find myself doing it," Tiana says grimly with teary eyes.

"I believe that's because he's your father, and you love him," Aiden says in consolation.

"Yeah, I believe so. I don't want to love him, but somehow, I am grateful to him for making me who I am. If not for my position and power, I wouldn't even have half the respect and reverence I have today, and it's all because of him," she says, wiping a tear from her eyes.

"Well, my mother used to say, '*no matter how much someone has helped you in this world, if they are becoming a thorn in your flesh, find the courage to leave. It can be hard, but I want you to know that you matter too, my son. You are my love*'," Aiden says, mimicking his mother.

Tiana sees how he mimics his mother and smiles. Aiden decides to impress her even further because he just made her smile. So, he makes a creature out of light and makes it appear before her. Tiana's happiness increases as she plays with the wings of the cat-like creature, smiling brighter than the sun outside. Aiden's heart is filled with so much love for her as he watches her play with the little creature

"You are more beautiful when you smile," he says, passionately staring at her.

"Thank you, Aiden, you are not bad yourself," she replies, returning his passionate stare.

CHAPTER 11

NEW QUESTIONS

Aiden and Dayan are at a healing class, about to learn how to heal things or reconstruct them using magic spells. Their instructor's name is Kilon, a commander in the third corps. Kilon has a sturdy physique. He has bushy eyebrows and a small beard that encircles his mouth. He is very strict, so he doesn't tolerate mistakes from his students. He's of the school of thought that he teaches quite well for everyone to understand him, so there's no reason to make mistakes. He often yells and keeps a stern face, and whenever he jokes, it's a snide remark at a person. This is just their third class with him, and the students already know his abrasive demeanor.

"Alright, class, our lesson today is bringing back a flower from a single stalk. As you can all see, there's a flower stalk in front of you, so I will teach you how to reconstruct it, bringing back its petals as though it was never dead," he says, peering through the still eyes of his students.

"So, to do this, you must first ensure your energy is balanced. After that, you'd move it from your body and concentrate on the finger you want to use to direct the energy. Please take note; you are to direct and not stress it. Once that is done, you'd say the words 'let all things be anew, like the coming of the day and night, and as the phoenix rises.' You repeat the words until you see the object reconstructing."

Kilon demonstrates as he speaks, causing the students to dazzle at how meticulous he brings back the flower, one piece at a time. After that, he instructs them to do theirs.

Everyone gets busy and starts casting their spells, channeling their energy as Kilon had instructed. The students shut out distractions to avoid errors. At the end of the exercise, some students get it right, and some don't, making their stalk explode in their faces. However, another stalk shows up when this happens. Dayan hits the air in excitement as he gets it right, even though it's his second attempt. He looks over to Aiden, who's having problems reviving his.

Aiden is trying vigorously to get his stalk up with its petals and beauty. He has gone over the process six times, and it's still not working. He looks around the class only to see almost everyone succeeding at their spells and wonders why his isn't working. He's surprised to see Tiana watching him, "how long has she been standing?" he asks himself. And in an attempt to impress her, he tries reconstructing the flower one more time, and he's amazed at how great the spell works out. He didn't only renew the flower, he made it into a bouquet, and everyone, even his teacher, Kilon, was astonished.

"Seems like your energy was way too balanced, Aiden," Kilon says to him.

"Yes," he says, smiling. He looks towards the window where Tiana was watching earlier and finds her smiling at him. He smiles back and even waves at her.

***

After the training, Aiden goes to Tiana's quarters to present the flower bouquet to her.

"This is a symbol of my love for you," he says

"Aww, thank you... I can't remember the last time I received flowers," Tiana says.

"I didn't even know you liked flowers, but I'm happy you do," Aiden says, moving towards her.

"Of course, I do, and I believe you wouldn't have done this if not for me," she teases him as she wraps her hand around him.

"Who says? I just needed a little motivation, that's all," Aiden retorts, pulling her closer to himself.

"Yeah, you do. And how did the motivation go?" Tiana continues teasing him.

"It—"

Aiden is interrupted by two men who barge into the room. He tries to challenge them, but Tiana holds him back.

"It's alright, Aiden. Give us some room, please," She begs.

"Are you sure?" he asks, looking suspiciously at the men.

"Yes, it's okay," she reaffirms

Aiden nods, leaving Tiana in the room with the unknown men.

"What do you want?" Tiana asks the men.

"It is time, Tiana," the man standing on the right side replies.

"Already?" she asks, perplexed.

***

Aiden is back in his room and can't stop thinking of the two mean-looking men who barged into Tiana's room earlier. His mind comes up with numerous possible reasons for their visit.

"Are you alright?" Dayan asks as he notices the worry in Aiden's eyes.

"Yes, I just need some air to cool my head," Aiden replies.

"Okay, man"

Aiden leaves the room to take a walk. It's late at night, and everyone is probably asleep except for some students who are up to no good. He teleports to the top of the building for a better view and soon notices some movement in a corner. He watches them closely and realizes that the walking figures aren't students. He takes a few minutes to think but comes up with nothing. He decides to follow them, as he can't alert anyone. The elders, generals, and other high-ranking officers often close their doors so that nobody can disturb them.

He sees the men bring down the patrolling officers one after the other before making their way to the weapons room. The weapons room is a chamber protected with highly protective spells. The room houses powerful, evil, and mystical objects, swords, spears, and amulets capable of destroying armies within minutes. Therefore, only the elders of the institute have spells and the power to open the room. Even then, they have to open all three doors to gain full access to the room.

"How do they think they'll open the doors?" Aiden asks and laughs within himself. He puts himself together as he follows them.

His eyes widen as one of the doors opens. He shakes his head in disbelief, moving closer to the building. As soon as he reaches hearing distance, someone apprehends him. The man knocks him down and reaches for his neck, trying to strangle him.

"You can see me?" Aiden asks in surprise. He'd used a spell to cloak himself from visibility, so how did this man find him?

"No, I can't, but I can feel your presence. I can feel any presence no matter how much spell is used to suppress it," the man boasts, still choking him.

Aiden quickly conjures an energy blast to shoot the man off him. He makes himself visible as soon as he gets the man away from him. The sorcerer at the door looks back for a moment before returning to work. After a while, two other men join the sorcerer at the door, and they all focus on Aiden.

"Who are you? And how were you able to open the doors to the weapons room?" Aiden questions them.

"There are things that are way too complex for you to comprehend, boy. In fact, you have seen way too much, leaving us with no choice but to kill you. But, as a show of honor, I shall tell you my name," the first man says.

"I don't need your name, you bastard," Aiden shouts.

"My name is Rodnik, and you shall eat those words," he says, pulling out a sword from under his black garment and dashing towards Aiden.

Aiden sees this and charges toward him, engaging him in a fight. Rodnik swings his sword at Aiden, who quickly dodges the attack with his shield. Rodnik lets his face fall in disappointment as he watches the boy dodge. He kicks Aiden's shield, sending him rolling through the ground. Rodnik jumps, aiming to land on Aiden, but the latter moves out of the way before he reaches him. Rodnik changes his attack strategy as he realizes that Aiden might not die if he continues his usual attack. He conjures a powerful blast that pushes Aiden to the floor. Seeing an opening, Rodnik sends his sword flying towards Aiden, who's now bleeding. Using all the strength in him, Aiden stops the swords in mid-air. Just then, something awakens in him, turning his eyes blue and raising his hair to the air. He starts to levitate as the sword before him crumbles to pieces. The sleeves of his shirt tear apart, and a crust begins to appear on his arms, covering his whole arms in gold markings of straight lines and circles symbolizing something.

Rodnik tries to attack, but Aiden waves his hand at him, releasing a wave of energy that hits and pushes him through a building nearby, knocking him out.

"It can't be, is he truly...?" one of the men with the sorcerer exclaims.

Seeing that Aiden will come for them, they vanish, leaving behind the sorcerer, who has gained access to the building. Aiden sends a wave of energy at them as they teleport to stop them. Unfortunately, it misses them, destroying where they were standing.

Moments later, the sorcerer comes out of the building to find his men on the floor. Aiden furrows his eyebrow upon seeing the sorcerer. He constructs a hand in his state of anger as he reaches for the sorcerer, crushing him. The sorcerer struggles to break free, sending attacks at Aiden, who counters everything.

"Aiden, stop; it's me," the sorcerer cries.

Aiden loses his grip as shock grips him.

"Who are you?" Aiden asks.

The sorcerer uses his magic to remove his mask, revealing his identity.

"It's me!"

Aiden's mouth opens in shock as he stares at the person before him. It takes a few minutes for him to regain himself. Finally, his eyes return to normal, and his blonde hair falls to his neck. He descends from the air and takes the hand away from the sorceress, making it vanish.

"Tiana!" he calls

Tiana gets up from the floor as she tries to regain her composure. She looks at the crest on Aiden's arms and tries to move toward him. However, she stops when she hears faint noises coming toward them. She knows they are fellow sorcerers, and it wouldn't be a welcoming party when they arrive. She looks at Aiden, who's waiting for an answer, and reaches for his hands.

"I will explain everything when I return, I promise," she says, kissing him before vanishing into the wind.

To Be Continued...In Book Two

Coming Late Summer 2022...